TALES FROM A MOUNTAIN

A Collection of Short Stories

EMIKAT JUN

Wrate's Publishing

First published in 2021 by Wrate's Publishing

ISBN 978-1-8383400-1-8

Copyright © 2021 by Emikat Jun

Edited and typeset by Wrate's Editing Services

www.wrateseditingservices.co.uk

A CIP catalogue record for this book is available from the British Library.

For all my Lolas (Romana, Martha, Rosa, Maria, Aurora, Corazon, and many others), who nourished my imagination when I was young with their storytelling. Thank you, and may you all be happy where you are now.

Contents

ONE

Roots in The Mountains

THEY FARMED HERE and they farmed there. In the mountains of the Cortillas, that was the way people survived for many centuries. Nobody knew how they started living there, for nothing of their early existence was ever recorded. Older folk talked about the legend of Ootah, where God, in his journey on earth, stopped for a rest and, due to his exhaustion, vomited on the spot at the top of the region's highest mountain. His spew formed a huge white rock that was visible from everywhere in the Cortillas.

When people worldwide heard about this they flocked to the mountain to pay tribute to God. Very few of the pilgrims succeeded, and the ones who did never made it back to their homeland. They had no choice but to survive in the mountains.

But there's another story that was passed on. Over 2000 years ago, a group of people called Indos, from across the oceans, followed their dream to find a better place to live. They braved crossing the seas in their wooden boats. Many perished during their journey, and those who made it to land found that other people had already settled along the shore.

The Indo people carried on with their journey further up into the mountains. With their skilful knowledge of hunting and jungle life, some managed to survive, and they began to settle in different places, gradually forming villages. Farming became their primary source of living, and continues to be so to this day.

In one of the mountain villages called Bolay, a farmer named Diego and his wife Ani were married, but several years on, Ani was yet to give birth to a child. The village was a close-knit community. A married couple without a child would be deemed unnatural, and whispers would pass around that the gods had punished the couple for their sinful past. The elders would also try to separate the couple on the grounds of being 'non childbearing'.

Eventually, Diego and Ani could no longer bear being taunted and ridiculed by their fellow villagers. One bright, moonlit night, they left the village centre, with their two carabaos towing their belongings. They trudged through to the woody hillside a few miles outside the village, before stopping to camp under a huge rock for the night.

The following day, after their breakfast of roasted sweet potatoes and poached eggs, which Ani prepared in a makeshift stove, Diego surveyed the surrounding area. He was slender and 5 ft 9 inches tall. At nearly forty years of age, his strong muscles were visible in his upper arms and calves. His brown skin was so dark that sometimes his thinly cut moustache went unnoticed. His hair was black and straight, and his nose was slightly turned up. His clear brown eyes gave a penetrating look that indicated his years of learning the land's rudiments.

As he trekked through luscious trees, shrubs and bushes,

he cut some of them with his sharp and elongated machete, making a passageway through the dense, wild vegetation. When not in use, he kept his machete inside its wooden, holster-like case, which he hung on the *rattan* belt around his waist. Wild fruits of berries and guavas abounded, and he'd pick and eat them as he fancied. When he'd almost reached the top of the sloping hill that branched off from a mountain's vast rainforest, his eyes gleamed as he discovered a stream with crystal clear water running through it. Overjoyed, he ran to the banks, tasted the water and then splashed it onto his face.

'Oh, all the gods in the heavens and on earth, I honour you. May you accept my most grateful and humble thanks?' he chanted.

He kneeled down and bent forward until his face touched the ground. After that, he followed the stream down to the treacherous terrain until he came to a spot eerie with a thundering noise. He watched in awe as the stream ended with a beautiful waterfall that cascaded a few hundred feet down towards a raging river.

Diego stood there mesmerised for a few minutes, before heading upstream and following his earlier passageway. He occasionally stopped listening to the birdsong and considered what was around the place to live on. At one point, he spotted what looked like a freshwater eel at the shallow end of the stream. He pondered over this for a moment, as eels were usually nocturnal. Could it be a snake? he wondered. He looked closer into the clear water and concluded that it was definitely an eel. The water came up to his knees as he gently stepped into it. He tried to catch the eel three times, but it managed to slip through his fingers on each attempt. It frantically struggled, and Diego finally knelt on it to keep it steady. He cut a bit from his rattan belt, tied the eel through its fins, wrapped it up in leaves and hung it over his belt.

As he continued on his trek, he passed abundant watercress and noticed many bamboos and *nipa palm* trees along the way. Diego decided that this was a place he and his wife could start to cultivate. By midmorning, he was back, and he eagerly told Ani what he had discovered and planned for them.

It took three days of hard work to clear a space in the woody landscape and build a *nipa hut* for their dwelling. On the first day, Diego cut trees, shrubs, bushes and wild plants with his machete and axe. Meanwhile, Ani cleared them away to first dry and then be burned. It was almost summer and the weather was dry, the temperature mild and the days longer. They worked until dusk, only stopping for their meal, which consisted of rice, watercress and grilled eel, thanks to Diego's earlier catch.

The following day, Diego gathered bamboos, rattan and the *nipa palm* leaves that grew abundantly near the stream. The carabaos towed the material to the cleared land, and by nightfall Diego and Ani started the foundations of their dwelling, putting up the four tree trunks they'd cut the previous day and using them as their main posts.

They woke at dawn and started working on the thatched roof, using the *nipa palm* leaves. By midday, they tied the bamboos together in sections to make up the walls with the rattan. By the end of the third day, their first dwelling was up, except for the bamboo floor that needed more time to finish; the bamboos had to be cut and split thinly and uniformly and tied more delicately. In the meantime, the earth was their floor.

They toiled each day until dusk, clearing more land and using the wood they'd cut down to improve their dwelling.

They started to cultivate the cleared land, and not long after that they built their first ricefield. First, they had to flatten the field. Diego whistled away while vigorously digging the ground using old pickaxes of varied sizes and shapes. Not far off and singing a few melodies of her own, Ani shovelled the excavated soil onto a wooden wheelbarrow and distributed it to even out the field.

Day in, day out, this was their back-breaking routine, which was only interrupted when Ani checked the time using her shadow. When she could hardly see it while standing under the sunlight, it was midday and she would head home to prepare their meal. Within a few weeks, they had dug an area big enough to plant rice to last them a year.

Diego had to irrigate the field with water from the stream. He did this by digging a small water canal. The water would soften the ground until it was ready to be ploughed, and it would continue to flow so that the plants on the ricefield could grow. Once the land softened, the couple methodically constructed a dike out of the mud around the edges of the ricefield, which kept the water within it. Rice seedlings were planted and harvested after five months.

Days, months and years passed; this was their life. They hardly left their farm, except for when Diego had to go to the village centre for supplies. He would barter some of their rice and vegetables for essential commercial goods such as salt, soap, cooking oil and clothing. On his first trip to the village centre, the villagers were all curious to know what had happened to him and Ani since they had moved on. Ani's distant cousin Mario showed particular interest. After a few chats, he invited Diego to his house and offered to buy the couple's old and neglected village house and farm. Diego accepted the offer and went back to his new farm with his supplies and a pair of cows, goats, pigs and chickens.

One day, the summer sun was unbearable and Diego and his carabaos took an earlier-than-usual break from ploughing. For his rest, Diego usually lay on his back under his favourite coconut tree and took a little snooze, while the carabaos ate the grass. This time, he decided to sit on the rock beside the tree.

As he examined the land around him, he realised that he and his wife had done an incredible amount in the space of five years. They had cultivated rice terraces consisting of seven ricefields and developed a small sugarcane plantation that produced at least three large, clay jars of the native wine *basi* each year. They also had some coffee plants and plenty of vegetable gardens in their backyard. Their dwelling was now a wooden, open-plan house. They had also amassed several more animals and now had dozens of chickens, a dozen pigs, five goats, three cows and five carabaos. Diego was still counting the animals in his head when he spotted movement in the nearby stream.

Diego was transfixed as he gazed at his naked wife taking a bath. It was a long time since he had noticed how beautiful she was, and despite being forty, her looks hadn't diminished. At this point, Ani was washing her long dark hair and rubbing soap onto her skin, oblivious to the fact she was being watched. Yes, her skin had roughened over the years of farming, and her fingers had gone very coarse. Wrinkles had formed on her once soft and tender face. But to Diego, she still carried the charming spirit that had attracted him when they'd first met during her cousin's wedding celebration.

At the time, Ani led a group of nine young women clad in colourful costumes. Together, they presented a highland dance called *palok*, accompanied by the tune of the percussion instrument *gongs*, which were played by nine men. Diego thought she was the most beautiful girl he had ever seen, as she confidently and gracefully moved her curvy figure with each step of the highland dance. At 5 ft 4 inches, she was the tallest in the girls' group. Her oval-shaped face lit up when she smiled, revealing a perfect set of teeth.

Diego was standing by the exit area when Ani passed by after her presentation. Their gaze met briefly, and Diego saw her striking, large, round brown eyes. For a split second, the sight melted him. By midnight, and after a few glasses of the native wine, he managed to dance with her as a local singer sang some old ballad music. The following summer, Ani and Diego were wed too.

Diego was suddenly interrupted from his reminiscing by a loud, trembling snort. He rushed to see what had surprised the heavy-weight animal; it appeared that one of the piglets had wandered from its pen and was hovering around the carabaos. Diego laughed out loud at the sight of this tiny piglet trying to get a feed from one of the enormous animals, mistaking it for the mother pig. He carefully ushered the piglet to a passageway towards its pen, and it made a squeaky *ngweek ngweek* noise as it ran away.

He gathered back the carabaos and happily whistled as he continued ploughing the ricefield. That night, with the kitchen stove's log fire dying out at the far corner of their house, Ani prepared their usual bed on the floor.

Nearly two harvest seasons had passed when one night, Ani felt extreme pain in her stomach. Diego immediately went to the village centre to fetch Sita, an elderly healer.

To the couple's delight, Ani gave birth to a healthy little boy. They named him Lukas.

TWO

Alda's Trek

'BY ALL MEANS, come back tomorrow morning,' whispered the ailing father to his thirteen-year-old daughter. The daughter nodded with a look of determined courage on her face. She pulled the blanket over to her father, tucked him in tightly, and made sure the jug of water by his bedside was full.

She rummaged through the tiny, dimly lit house for her thickest sweater and reached for the overworn jacket that hung on the back of the door. She wrapped herself up as warmly and as comfortably as she could manage. She needed a torch. She found an empty rum bottle, made sure it was dry inside and filled it with kerosene. Tearing some sheets of paper from her old school notepad, she rolled them tightly up together. She could hear her father desperately coughing as she inserted the roll into the bottle. Once her homemade torch was ready, she tilted the bottle to soak the paper with kerosene and then lit it with a matchstick before carefully putting the matchbox in her pocket. She went to her father's side, touched his forehead and said, 'I'll be back, *ama*.' As she left, she closed the door gently behind her.

≈

Alda and her ageing father lived on an isolated village farm called Lannok. Her mother died giving birth to Alda, and her father had raised her on his own. He never remarried and had devoted his life to his daughter, his only child. Despite being isolated, Alda still went to school and would start secondary school the following term.

Their nearest neighbour was five miles away in the village town, and his house could only be reached on foot. It was 10 pm. Outside the house, Alda gathered her thoughts; every footstep she would make would be crucial. She began her trek of the rugged paths to the village town to get some help. She wished the moon was friendlier tonight – it seemed the universe's elements were conniving against her.

Holding a wooden walking stick in her right hand, which doubled as her weapon, Alda clutched her torch tightly with her left hand, as if her journey depended on it.

As she trudged through the woody hills, she could hear the noise of wild creatures: the hissing snakes, the *koraa-koraa* of the monkeys and the owls conversing in their strange ways. She thought about a rock suddenly falling off the cliff above the footpath and crashing her into oblivion, or she would misjudge the path and step onto a precipice, or – her biggest fear – a snake would be waiting to jag its venom into her bare feet.

But she had no time to be scared; her feet kept moving, mindless of the jaggy bits of stone on her way. Tonight, she occupied her thoughts with her purpose.

Alda could sense that she was nearing the village town,

as the dirt track she was following turned into a wider path. Soon enough, she was knocking at the door of the village's only nurse.

'Who is that?' a groggy sounding man called from inside.

'It's Alda, from Lannok, Mr Tanod,' Alda replied slowly and in a contained voice, as she didn't want to rouse the neighbours. The door immediately flung open, and Mr Tanod let her in.

'Alda, why are you here alone and so late?' he asked.

'My father is not well at all. He's been feeling poorly for the last few days, and today he did not go to the farm, as he said he needed some rest. He was in bed all day. When I came home from the ricefields, he was breathless. He insisted he would feel better after a few hours, but he only got worse. I can't bear seeing him that way; he was never unwell like that before.' Alda started to sob. 'I had to put a wet towel on his forehead as he was hot, and I think his temperature was very high. Would you be able to come with me tonight and check on him? Please, Mr Tanod?' Alda pleaded.

'Alda, my wife is heavily pregnant, and she could give birth at any time. No one else is here to care for her just in case . . .' Mr Tanod stammered.

'Oh, I see. It's OK if you can't come with me tonight, but can you give me some medicines to take home, please?' Alda felt disappointed but understood the nurse's predicament.

'Why don't you stay here for tonight and I'll get somebody early tomorrow to stay with my wife. We can both go back to see your father,' Mr Tanod suggested.

'No, I cannot do that. I must go back to my father tonight. He needs me and some medicines.'

Mrs Tanod woke up and joined them in the living room.

'Maybe my sister Marlyn is still awake next door; why don't you see if she can come and stay with me for tonight?' she suggested to her husband after hearing Alda's story.

Mr Tanod went out and Mrs Tanod offered Alda some biscuits and coffee, which she gratefully accepted.

A few minutes later, Mr Tanod and Marlyn came in. It didn't take long for Mr Tanod to prepare all his medical equipment and medicines; then, with a quick goodbye to his wife and Marlyn, he and Alda started their trek back to Lannok.

This time, they used a big torchlight to light their path.

As they reached the house, Alda and Mr Tanod could hear the rooster's crows. 'Is . . . that . . . that you, Alda?' Her father mumbled, and he was gasping for breath when they came in.

'Yes, *ama*, Mr Tanod is here with me, and we've got some medicines for you,' Alda replied as she and Mr Tanod walked inside her little house. Though very exhausted, she managed to sound cheerful.

As Alda poured water into a tin cup and assisted the nurse, her father said, 'Thank you very much, Mr Tanod, for coming over . . . and what would I do without you, my dear child?' Her father's voice was weak and cracking.

'Don't worry, Mr Malaga, you will be fine,' Mr Tanod reassured the elderly gentleman, as he completed taking his temperature and blood pressure.

Alda smiled; her tiredness seemed to vanish just as the creeping sunrise was swallowing the darkness of the night.

THREE

The Little Mound

EROL WAS a fifth-grader in elementary school. At twelve
years old, he should have been in his first year at high
school, but he was a slow learner. Apart from being the
eldest in his class, at 5ft 2 inches, he was also the tallest. He
wore the same brown trousers to school every day, and he
had done for the last two years. They were now totally worn
out and only reached halfway down his calves, exposing his
light brown skin. His Spartan-made blue flip-flops had small
holes on each heel. His hair was straight, black and cut in a
bob style, and his eyes were a very dark brown.

It was lunch break at school, and Erol avoided the queue
for the toilets by the main building. He was fed up with
being pushed to the back every time he went there. The
other children repeatedly told him that because he was the
tallest, he should always be the last in the queue. He went to
the back of the school building, down past the playground
area, and hid behind the bushes to urinate. As he finished
and moved out of the bushes, something on the ground

caught his attention. It was a little mound made of reddish soil, and it was sticking up in the middle of the grass.

'Pweest, pweeeest pweeeeest.'

The whistling was very high-pitched. Erol thought that yet again some of his classmates were playing tricks on him. A gentle beating of drums ensued, coupled with a flash of lights above the little mound. Curiosity got the better of him, and Erol followed the flickering lights as they left the mound and moved further downhill, following a rugged and bushy path. He soon entered a dense forest. Giant leafy trees towered over him, darkening the whole area. The flickering lights got brighter against the darkness, and the beating of the drums became louder and more melodic. Erol could hear voices but he couldn't make out the words. He carried on walking until he reached a bright area.

When he stepped on it, a big hole opened up in front of him, and he glimpsed a vast stairway leading down to a glittering area below. He stood for a while, uncertain of what to do. The drums suddenly stopped, and the place was very still and quiet. He felt his trousers being pulled from the hem and, glancing down, he jumped with horror, as he saw three *ancicets* – little beings – almost hanging at the bottom part of his trousers. They were a diminutive size, only coming up to Erol's knees, and they had round, yellow faces. Erol moved back, but they stared at him with their big greyish eyes; it was a welcoming look. Their one-holed noses were big and pointy, which almost made their thin-lipped mouths invisible. Their ears had the shape of a button mushroom, and they were clad in orange jumpsuits, with their heads wrapped in brown scarves.

They repeatedly chanted in an extraordinary and incomprehensible language. Astonished, Erol followed them, and when his feet touched the first step of the stairway, everything around him glistened with gold. The drums restarted with an echoing sound and a more upbeat tone. Erol noticed that each end of each step held a golden jar; the lower the step, the larger the jar.

The bottom of the stairway gave way to an enormous hall glittered with gold. To the right side of the aisle was a long dining table complete with plates and cutlery. The high back chairs were elaborately carved with figures of all sorts of animals, trees and fruit. To the left was the dance floor with benches lining the walls. Everything was made of gold, except for the massive diamond chandelier that hung at the centre of the ceiling. And in the middle of the hall was the largest of the golden jars, which occupied a fifth of the room. Under its faucet were cups lined up according to their size. The place was most beautiful but eerie, and Erol began to feel uneasy.

A deep thundering voice echoed through the hall.

'W-E-L-C-O-M-E!'

Erol was now trembling with fear. He looked down at the three *ancicets*; the voice hadn't come from them. The first one just smiled and waved up to him. The second was nodding, and the third was shaking its head. He looked around as he moved towards the centre of the hall. He could only see the three little beings with him, but he felt like hundreds were watching. Where had the voice come from?

He looked at the big jar and remembered what his grandfather used to tell him: if you are naughty, the *ancicets* will come and get you and then cook you in a giant jar! Erol was now in a real panic. Then he noticed a tiny window at the far left corner of the hall. He ran towards it, and the third *ancicet* followed him. As he approached the window, the being caught Erol's attention, and he squatted down to its level. Erol offered his hand, but it reached for his pocket instead, before abruptly disappearing. Perplexed, Erol stood up and went to the window. He stuck his head out and felt like he was being lifted.

Suddenly, he was standing on the spot where he had relieved himself earlier, but the little mound was no longer there. He shook his head to clear his mind. When he looked around, he noticed the playground and remembered his afternoon class. He started to run towards it.

It was nearly three o'clock when he arrived at the door of his classroom. His teacher was standing by the door with a stern look on his face. When he noticed Erol, he quickly instructed the other pupils to finish their exercises quietly, while he was away for a few minutes. Erol's face was covered with sweat, and he was out of breath as he stood in front of his teacher. The teacher summoned Erol to follow him to the principal's office.

Erol was extremely nervous. In between stammers, he began to relate in detail his strange adventure to his teacher and the principal, who were both sceptical. They said Erol had gone to sleep during his lunch break, had a bad dream and hadn't heard the school bell. The principal told Erol that she needed to speak to his parents the following day. At that point, Erol started to cry and he put his hands in his pockets.

He felt something round in one of them, and as he brought it out, he found himself staring at a huge, pure gold coin. He lifted it in astonishment to show his teacher and the principal, who stared in disbelief.

Erol handed the object to the principal, and as she held it in her palm, it slowly became smaller, until it vanished.

The two baffled adults looked at each other and then at Erol.

That week, rumours spread around the school about Erol's *anting-anting*, or magic coin, and he soon gained many friends, who did not tire of listening to his story.

FOUR

Sleepover at Lola Kony's

Rita asked her parents if she could go to a sleepover on Friday with her cousins at *Lola* Kony's house. They agreed, as long as she completed all her chores at home in the week and did well with her school homework.

It was Friday, and Rita was so excited. She hopped and whistled as she walked the fifteen-minute distance from the village centre school to her house. Rita saw a dragonfly by the side of the path and stopped. She tiptoed towards the leaf it was sitting on. As she tried to catch its tail with her right thumb and finger, it hurried off in a graceful glide over to the other side of the path. Rita chased it. The dragonfly glided from one side of the walkway to the other and leapt onto different leaves, as if teasing Rita.

Rita had always been fascinated with dragonflies. Whenever she saw one, she would not pass it until she touched it, and this time, she was as determined as ever. She thought the dragonfly was huge, and with its green, blue, yellow and red colours, it was beautiful too.

She could hear the voices of other pupils behind her.

'Shhh . . . stay where you are! Don't move. I have to catch this one. It's such a beauty.'

They all knew Rita, and what she said mattered to them. Since first grade, she had been top of her class, and now in sixth grade, the pupils had voted her as the president for their elementary school. They all sat down on the path and waited. Rita sat on a little rock on one side of the walkway for a few minutes, observing how long the dragonfly stayed on one leaf before moving onto another. She then slowly moved ahead onto the other side of the path, waiting patiently until she finally captured the creature.

She put it on her left hand and half-cupped it with her right, as all the kids surrounded her. As usual, she studied it – the insect had six legs, the head was a third of the body size, it had a very long, bluish tail, and two long yellowish wings on each side. Its body was blue and green, and its stomach was red. The bulgy head was black, with a pair of shiny, clear eyes.

The other kids shared their excitement and wonder.

'Wow!'

'Beautiful!'

'Look at the different colours.'

'What big eyes.'

'It's got six legs!'

'Doesn't it sting you, Rita?'

'Oh no, I wouldn't touch that.'

'Have you all finished? It needs to go now,' Rita said, as she fully opened her palm to let the creature go.

'What took you so long, Rita?' her mother asked as she came through the front door.

'Oh, just this dragonfly I passed by . . .'

'Mmmm, don't tell me you tried to catch it again.'

'Oh yes, mama.'

'Now, you've still got chores to do. The dishes need washing before dinner. There are two empty plastic jugs in the kitchen to be filled with drinking water, too'.

'Aw, why did Ana not do the dish washing? Why is it always me?'

'Ana is not well; that's why she didn't go to school today, remember?'

Rita went to change in the bedroom that she shared with her younger sister. She glanced at Ana, who was lying in bed

'So, you cannot go to *Lola* Kony's tonight?' she asked Ana, who shook her head.

'Could you tell me all about it when you come back, please?' Ana pleaded, and Rita nodded before rushing to the kitchen.

She gathered the dirty dishes on a little washbasin, which she carried on her head as she walked towards the spring well about two hundred yards from the house. As she washed and rinsed the dishes, she wondered what was in store at *Lola* Kony's that night. She made another trip to the spring well to get some drinking water. Dinner was ready when she arrived back home.

Lola Kony was a sixty-year-old widow who lived alone in Rita's village, which housed at least ten families. Her two grown-up daughters lived in neighbouring towns with their own families and would occasionally visit her. She was a

village catechist and she visited Rita's school three days a week to give lessons on religion. She was a distant relation of Rita's mother, but she was almost a real grandmother to Rita and her cousins in the village. A gifted storyteller, Rita, her sister and cousins would often go for a sleepover to listen to her most exciting and fascinating tales.

Lola Kony's wooden house was tiny, with three parts. First, you'd climb up four wooden steps to enter her kitchen. This led to the living room and bedroom, which had one small bed in the corner. That night, Rita and her two cousins, Naty and Lita, arrived for their sleepover. As *Lola* Kony tidied up her kitchen and prepared for the night, the three girls sat on the floor in the living room and listened intently to the drama programme being aired on the transistor radio.

Once *Lola* Kony turned the radio off, they lay side by side on the floor, which was cushioned with thick blankets. *Lola* Kony lay on the small bed. As usual, before starting the story, they all knelt and prayed.

'Long before the Spaniards colonised the country and brought Christianity to the land during the 16th century,' began *Lola* Kony. '*Kabunian* was the God of the gods, and there were three main deity beliefs amongst the people in the mountains: nature spirits, the *kakarading* (dead ancestors and relatives) and mythological heroes.

'During those days, a couple and their eight-year-old son, Tamayo, lived in a small, isolated village. They survived by farming and hunting. One day, the father came home from hunting in the adjacent hill forest. He became very ill. After a few days, a medium came to perform a *dawak*, a healing rite on him, for illness and death was attributed to vengeful spirits.'

Upon hearing 'spirits', Naty and Lita shrieked. 'This is scary, *Lola*,' they said.

'No, it's not,' Rita butted in. 'It's fascinating. So, what happened to the boy, Tamayo, then?' She sat up and leaned against the wall.

'We'll come to that eventually,' said *Lola* Kony, before continuing. 'Well, the night before the medium arrived, some men, his father's hunting mates, came for merriment, to appease the spirits. They performed the highland dance *salisid* and played the *tungatong* with gongs. The house was a small, wooden open-plan abode with a firewood stove in the far corner. Tamayo's father was lying on the floor in the corner opposite the fire, while the men made their merriment.

'The following day, before the medium arrived, Tamayo's mother and relatives decorated the four corners of the house with ferns. A chicken was butchered for sacrifice, and the medium assessed the liver of the sacrificial animal, to see whether it was a good or a bad omen. She shook her head and wailed.

'The next day, the father died. It appeared that he must have stepped unknowingly into an old burial cave, without acknowledging or making appeasement with the spirits that lived there.

'People from the neighbouring villages came over for the father's burial. Some of them were his fellow hunters.

'Your *ama* was a courageous man. He was a skilful hunter and the best we ever had here in the region. He could kill a boar with just one sharp hit with his bow and arrow. We will miss him very much. I hope you grow up to be just like him, boy!' said the bearded hunter, as he tapped Tamayo on the shoulder. Tamayo listened gladly, as each man shared stories of their meaningful times with his father while in the forests.

'The medium performed the burial ritual and the villagers took the body to the rocky cave near the top of the hill. It was tied to a chair in a sitting position and left there openly to fulfil its duty of protecting its family forever.

'Two years after his father died, Tamayo was gathering firewood one morning in the nearby forest, when he unknowingly passed the burial cave. When his father's body was taken there, he had not been allowed to come.

'He suddenly fell off a cliff. By the afternoon, his worried mother went looking for him. As she passed by the burial cave, she bowed and asked the spirits for permission to pass by, and for their help to find her son.

'Just as she straightened up to walk, a colourful dragonfly landed on her left shoulder and sat there for a few minutes. It then gently glided over to the little leaves ahead of her. Instinctively, she followed it towards the side of a cliff and started climbing down it. The mother found Tamayo sitting crying at the bottom. The cliff was so high, and it was a joyful shock for the mother to find that Tamayo was unhurt. She hugged him, as she asked him what had happened.

'In between sobs, he said, "I'm sorry, *ina*; I was following this trek, and all of a sudden, I stepped onto this precipice. I couldn't remember anything until I landed on a very soft spot. I couldn't find a way to climb back up."

'The mother looked around, but the dragonfly she had followed earlier was no longer there. She smiled and murmured, "thank you."'

By the time *Lola* Kony had finished the story, Rita was still sitting up, while the other two girls were fast asleep.

'*Lola*, do burial caves still exist?' she asked nervously.

'Not anymore, Rita. Those days are long gone. We now bury our dead in tombs in our backyards, or in the cemetery,' *Lola* Kony explained.

'Are dragonflies good spirits, then?' she asked.

'An excellent question, Rita,' *Lola* Kony replied. 'I'd like to presume so.'

In the darkness of the room, Rita smiled.

FIVE

Revisiting Lobo

Iт's twenty years ago since I last visited the village of Lobo, which I have been fond of since childhood. My mother had ricefields in the area, which relatives tended to. Every weekend, my siblings and I would hike down from the town centre and back up again to collect some of the produce for our weekly supply. As in most of the mountain villages, even in the twenty-first century, there was no transportation. Everyone moved around on foot.

Mother's ricefields had been sold off over the years, but our relatives still lived in the close-knit community that I had grown to love and cherish. From the town centre, it took half an hour to hike down the mountain to Lobo, and the uphill return journey took a further hour.

Nothing much had changed along the rugged footpath, except for a few cemented steps on the otherwise steep slopes. As I descended the mountain, the summer sun kept me profusely sweating. When the village came into view, I couldn't believe what I was seeing. Where once beautifully crafted nipa huts, clusters of wooden houses, with shiny, corrugated tin roofs now greeted my eyes. I felt a pang in my heart as I realised I might be going to a familiar but unrecognisable place.

Well, I thought to myself, *what should I expect after twenty years? Of course people had moved on, as they do everywhere else in the world, and just like I had!*

Nostalgia enveloped me, as I stood at a viewing point for a few minutes, conjuring my happy childhood memories of the place. I had heard there'd been lots of changes in the village. I guess technology and materialism had reached even the remotest areas of the world. As I entered the village, people looked out from their windows and acknowledged my presence. Kids, urged by their parents, ran to the house of my mother's aunt – whom we fondly called *ina Kib-os* – for being an elderly grandmother or relation, to tell her I was coming. The village had grown from having about two dozen houses to about a hundred, and not a single one of them was a nipa hut. There was now a village hall in the plaza centre, where we used to play volleyball and kick-the-can games.

It was midday on a Sunday, and almost everyone was at home after the church service at the village hall. A few women were doing their everyday chores, such as pounding rice outside their houses and tidying the vegetable gardens in their backyards. Somehow, I was glad their way of life had not changed much, despite the village's general outside appearance. Children ran about barefoot, and people welcomed me with smiles.

Ina was outside her house, waiting for me as I reached the centre of the village. She was about seventy years old and looked tinier than before, as her back formed a hunchback due to years of farming. But as she stood by the stairs outside her house, she looked fit and steady.

'Oh, it's so good to see you again, Beng,' she said, her face lighting up.

When I was a child, her house was raised on wooden stilts and divided into two parts. The kitchen consisted of a nipa hut with a *bansag*, or floor made of interwoven bamboos, which made the place a lot cooler during the summer months. It was reasonably spacious, with a wooden fire stove in the right-hand corner. This area of the house was the central gathering place, where the family ate their meals together on the floor. Most of them slept side by side on the floor in this room, where the fire stove's warmth made it feel cosy.

I certainly loved the times I slept here beside *ina*, listening to her folk tales until I fell asleep. A door led to the other section of the house, which consisted of two small bedrooms and a spacious living room that led to a porch with wooden benches. This area of the house wasn't used on a daily basis, but it was an important space for visitors when there were occasions in the village, such as weddings or other special gatherings.

As *ina* ushered me inside the kitchen, I noticed the wooden floor and the extension at the back. It looked like a proper wooden house now; the only thing that reminded me of the nipa hut was the wooden fire stove, which remained neatly intact in the corner. Bunches of unprocessed rice grains had been hung to dry above the stove, as they did before. The other part of the house remained the same. Although the appearance of the house from both the outside and the inside was very different since I last visited, I felt the same pleasing and relaxing atmosphere.

No sooner had people started to crowd into *ina*'s house, word spread that a visitor had arrived in the village. Everyone was eager to hear about the world I now lived in, and they took it in turns to look through the photo albums I had brought with me. In this part of the world, most people believed that anyone from the West had come from America. It was a bit of a struggle to explain that Scotland was not in America.

The kids were delighted when I gave them the candies I had brought with me. Some of the folks I'd played with when I stayed at *ina*'s house as a child now had their children and grandchildren with them, and it was hard trying to remember each of them as they were introduced.

Ina had her son-in-law butcher a chicken for our lunch, which I objected to and said was unnecessary. I explained I'd only come to say hello and wouldn't stay long.

'Don't be silly, this is what we do here when somebody visits,' *Ina* said, her tone almost a reprimand.

With my bare hands, I enjoyed eating our lunch of stewed chicken, rice, vegetables and fruits. The food was nicely spread out on trays and plates on the kitchen floor, and we sat on the floor as we ate.

It was strange having people sitting around us and watching as we tucked in, but they also listened to and joined in with our conversations. They were invited to eat but declined; they were just happy to come over and be part of the little gathering.

The meal was over, and everyone had a cup of coffee. We spoke about the changes I'd noticed since the last time I was here. I wondered if farming was doing much better than before, to help create the larger houses. They explained that most men and women nowadays found extra help financially by going to a goldmine mountain, which was an eight-hour trek away, in between the planting and harvesting seasons.

In the last three decades, the people who'd found the

goldmine fought off commercial business interests and kept it open for the region's locals. They would pay minimal fees to mine as much as they could. When villagers were lucky, they would return with tens or hundreds of kilograms of gold, which they sold and used to improve their houses or send their children to college.

It was a precarious livelihood, with miners using just the essential tools to dig tunnels inside the earth. Stories were told of a few villagers who'd lost their lives digging the tunnels or being buried underneath them. It was a sad reality, but the villagers were resilient to these occurrences, which, however challenging and tragic, were accepted as part of life. They wouldn't stop them from going back and forth to the goldmine.

Everyone joined in and alternately relayed past and present news or told stories. At one point, *ina* recalled the time when she took me to their *uma*, her family's large vegetable garden at the top of the opposite mountain, when I was about ten years old. She proudly declared that I was the bravest and strongest child at the time, as I carried home about ten reasonably sized squashes or pumpkins. She hadn't been back to the garden since her husband died ten years earlier. None of her eight children would dare do the climbs during the seven-hour trek to tend the garden and stay in the tiny adjoining nipa hut for days or sometimes weeks on end.

Noticing it was almost five o'clock in the afternoon, I found myself saying a regretful goodbye to everybody and promised to return in the future. Everyone in *ina Kib-os'* house was quick to say they enjoyed my visit and wished that their relations living in other parts of the country and the world would come back more often, even for just a short visit. They also reminded me not to forget them. For them, my visit provided a connection to an outside world with a life entirely alien to their own. I enjoyed my short stay so much that leaving the village at that moment made me emotional.

'OK, *ina*, I must go now before it gets dark. I hope to see you again soon. Take care always.'

I was teary as I hugged her tiny, thin figure.

'No, Beng, *you* take care,' she said with emphasis. 'Do not worry about us. We are just here; nothing bothers us except the weather sometimes. But it's you and the rest of our relations in the cities or other countries that we worry about. You live so far away, travelling on different forms of transport and living and mingling with strangers. You are always open to dangers that we only hear about and don't experience. I think you need to take good care always, my dear. Yes, I do hope I will still be here the next time you visit, Beng. God bless you always.'

Ina Kib-os walked with me until I reached the step going out of the village.

SIX

Wake Up Call

I was born in a *nipa* hut, a small, cosy abode with walls made of well-patched bamboo stems and roofs made of long, dried grassy strands. I spent my early years playing in the woods, and nature taught me life as it should. When I started school, I walked, hopped, jumped and ran past the forest to greet my friends. I pointed to and counted endless trees along the way. Breathing all that fresh air gave me so much pleasure.

I was encouraged to gain knowledge, so I went to college, but nothing prepared me for the changes that the city would bring. I became a successful engineer and worked for a timber company. I travelled across the globe earning more money than I could ever have dreamed of.

But I squandered it, and I felt the most profound regret when I realised this.

'Nobody's perfect,' I consoled myself.

I altered my goals and chose more satisfactory roles. I went back to my lovely village. It was too late. Nothing was left; it had all been buried, swept away by mudslides and entombed in rocks. And the trees in the forest were all gone.

SEVEN

The Voice

For the past couple of weeks, I had not been my usual, well-organised self. I was in denial for a very long time and avoided dealing with *it*. But the dreadful night when I was nine years old kept coming back to me, replaying like a broken record.

I hear it again, calling my name in such a familiar but strange voice, but I am dead. I'm supposed to be dead! Why do I hear things? I should just be . . . feeling them. Well, I guess I am not that dead.

My father used to tell me: 'My dear Victoria, you must always remember that there's a reason for everything and everything has a reason.'

I never understood it at the time, but somehow, I sensed its significance.

Yes, my father, my dearest father. He was not just the best lawyer in the city, with many awards under his belt after winning various high-profile cases, he was also the most loving and gentle person you could ever meet. My mother, brother and I adored him.

It was around 10 pm, and I was sitting on my bed

writing in my diary, when suddenly there was an almighty bang downstairs, followed by a rush of footsteps and doors banging here and there. I sat still, as I wondered what was going on. I knew my mother and father were in bed, and that my brother would no doubt already be fast asleep. Confused and frightened by the unusual banging noise, I turned off my bedside lamp.

I heard footsteps coming up the stairs, and then . . .

Bang! Bang! Bang!

The shooting was deafening. I jumped off my bed and crawled under it. I was shaking. I tried to call my mum and dad, but no words came out.

My door was kicked wide open and a torch flicked across my bedroom, as I heard two pairs of heavy boots on my floor. Then a husky, masculine-voiced person said, 'Empty!'

I heard my door close and started to sob. There was another shot, then . . . nothing. I woke up with uniformed police officers around me and commotion everywhere. I could barely make out the word 'hospital'.

When I was discharged from the hospital, I had to choose who to live with. It was between a childless aunt who lived a pretentious but glamorous life in the city and an uncle who had three kids and resided in a mountainous province. I chose the latter.

I had met Uncle Wildy, Aunt Thelma and my cousins, Anabelle, Wilma and Edgar during the few times that Father took us to their village, Balayo, in the province of Aplaya, for the weddings and birthdays of relatives, and for town fiestas. Although they lived in a humble farmhouse in the mountains, which was nothing like my father's upmarket townhouse in the city, I felt at ease.

I eventually settled down with my new family. My cousins were great, especially the oldest, Anabelle, who was a year older than me. At first, I missed my own family so much, and I often hid at the back of the house and wept. Anabelle would come and find me and then sit on the ground beside me until I stopped crying.

I also missed my toys, as well as the shopping malls and restaurants we used to go to as a family. In contrast, our primary recreation was playing in the backyard of the house. We also roamed the nearby fields, which I eventually became accustomed to.

One summer, my cousins and I played a game. We went to the huge, old star apple tree in the back garden and competed to climb the highest branch and gather as much of the ripe fruit as possible.

I followed Anabelle, as she cuddled the tree and stepped on the cut-out bark. She pushed herself up until she was able to hop onto the first big branch. Wilma and Edgar followed suit.

Anabelle explained what to do. Once you got onto the first branch, the trick was to reach for the leaves on the next upper branch, pull it down, and lift yourself onto it, just like monkeys do! It was tricky at first, but no sooner had I got the hang of it, I started to enjoy the climb and the star apples I had picked. I kept the ones I didn't eat in the pockets of my jumper.

The rule was that whoever reached a branch first would be able to pick all its fruit. I spotted one at the very top of the tree with dozens of ripe apples. And, with a newfound bravado, I went for it. But the branch was thinner and swayed with my weight. As I looked down at the thirty-foot drop, I started to panic. I called to my cousins below, who couldn't do anything to help me down.

'Hold on there, Victoria!' shouted Anabelle. 'Edgar will go and fetch Papa from the ricefields.'

Edgar quickly climbed down the tree and ran away to get his father. Anabelle and Wilma climbed down, too. This time, I was in tears. Petrified of falling, I clung to the trunk of the tree. Every time I put my feet on the branch, I could hear it crack.

'Throw down the apples in your pockets, and we'll catch them for you,' called Anabelle.

I hesitated, as it was awkward and dangerous to move, but my jumper was bulky and the apples were getting crushed. Slowly, I managed to empty my pockets of eleven apples.

Uncle Wildy finally arrived half an hour later. Anabelle was the oldest and got the brunt of his reprimand. He then calmly took the bamboo ladder and climbed up the apple tree, before gently assisting me down. He cautioned us all not to climb the tree again. Much embarrassed, I meekly nodded.

I grew very fond of Uncle Wildy and his family. They always treated me equally, as one of their own. Uncle Wildy told me on a few occasions how much he also missed my father, who was his big brother. One Sunday afternoon, after we all came back from the church, he and I sat together on the porch.

'You know, Victoria, your father was a courageous and determined man,' Uncle Wildy said. 'He always fought for what he believed was right. Even when we were young, he sometimes got into trouble with his teachers because he spoke his mind.'

He paused and lit his tobacco pipe. 'You know as well as

I do that God never sleeps. I believe and continue to pray that the people responsible for the deaths of him and your mother and brother will eventually be brought to justice. If only I could do something to make that happen sooner.'

His usually calm face grew grim and revealed wrinkles in his forehead and around his eyes. He inhaled and exhaled from his pipe and looked up absently at the sky.

When I finished high school, I had to leave the village and only went back for occasional visits. My cousins were devastated when I first left.

'Oh, we will miss you so much!' cried Anabelle. 'Don't forget our promise to write to each other when we meet our first boyfriend,' she whispered, and I nodded as I embraced my best friend.

'I know you are a fearless girl like your father; remember when you climbed that tree?' Uncle Wildy smiled and hugged me tight, just like how my father used to.

With the trust fund that my parents left, I went to study at the State University and became a lawyer.

A knock on my office door startled me.

'Ma'am Victoria, there's a phone call for you; they won't tell me who they are,' my secretary said, popping her head in.

'Thank you, Grace, put them on.'

'Hello Attorney Bayani, this is the Metropolitan Police Commissioner. We have been trying to contact you for the last two weeks. Your Uncle Wildy Bayani gave us your number.' There was a brief pause on the other line. 'There has been a major development in your father's case. Two of the prisoners serving the death penalty for another crime have confessed. If you could come down to the police headquarters as soon as possible, we will discuss it further.' The male voice on the other line was deep and authoritative.

'Yes, sir, I will be there in an hour. Thank you for your call.'

I couldn't control my excitement and apprehension. Two decades on, there was a prospect that I was going to face the killers of my family.

I quickly got ready and briefly explained to my secretary where I was going. I arrived at the police headquarters fifteen minutes early. I was wearing a smart navy suit dress and my long black hair was neatly tied up in a bun. I was aware that my face looked a bit pale; I could have done more with my make-up. I tried in vain to conceal my tired brown eyes from many sleepless nights with a pair of silver, thin-rimmed eyeglasses. At 5ft 6 inches tall, my three-inch black heels made me feel as tall as some of the officers in the building.

The commissioner looked older than I thought he'd be. He would be about my father's age, if he had lived. He was tall and stout, bespectacled and had grey hair. His blue, bemedalled uniform showed his power, but despite his authoritative presence, he was friendly. He ushered me into a room with two of his colleagues. There were documents and old photos on the table.

He then patiently explained to me that my father, Alberto Bayani, was the prosecutor in the Labanos versus Maginto case, involving two rival clans from one of the country's islands. Labanos had a strong case against Maginto, who was accused of killing a dozen Labanos supporters in their fight to control their island. After my father's death, nobody was able to pursue the case for fear of their own lives. To this date, it remained unsolved, as was the case involving my family.

'The two men who confessed were Maginto's right-hand men at the time,' the commissioner explained. 'However, Maginto and his accomplices were convicted of the murder of the leader and five supporters of another rival clan. They were sentenced to the death penalty. Now, are you aware that their punishment will be carried out next month?'

I was astonished. Maginto's name had made headlines on the news recently, with a public debate on the death penalty. Since then, there had been non-stop demonstrations, both for and against abolishing capital punishment.

I nodded.

'Well, what I need to ask you is this: do you want to re-open the case regarding the murder of your family? We will have to apply for the punishment of the convicted men to be rescheduled until your family's case is determined.'

The commissioner was looking me in the eye. 'I understand you are in a state of shock just now, but you have until tomorrow to let us know.'

There was a long pause, as I tried to take everything in.

'Sir, thank you so much for letting me know about all of this. I have decided that I do not wish to re-open my family's case. There is no point. Let their punishment be.'

That night, I wrote a very emotional letter to my Uncle Wildy. And for the first time in many years, I enjoyed a perfect night's sleep, uninterrupted by the voice calling my name.

EIGHT

The Interviewee

THE COUNCIL, led by Apo Kushak, the Supreme, and assisted by the ten mentors, interviewed the three remaining newcomers. The main agenda of this interview was to determine the fate of the three members, who had arrived six months ago and still needed to show more commitment in order to enter the next level of their development.

The first interviewee was Estela.

'Your honour, my Majesty, it took me a while to commit myself because I missed my family so much and couldn't leave the house. My daughter was always crying, my son was furious and my husband didn't know what to do. I had to watch over them twenty-four hours a day and assist them in their daily undertakings. But they have adjusted slowly to my absence and have started to accept that I can no longer be with them. I am now ready to move onto my next level.'

The second interviewee, Bisao, moved forward.

'Your honour, my Majesty, I was trapped in the rubble of a building during the war with the rebels. My fellow soldiers found my body only recently, and my family, who were so sad but relieved, have made the proper burial for me. I am now ready to move onto my next level.'

And the third interviewee, Cushapo, marched in.

'Well, your honour, my Majesty, I do not know why I am here now. I should be sitting at the top of my tree, watching what goes on around the world, especially the children playing. I dare not miss any of it! I've never seen anything before, except inside the womb of my mother. So now, can I go?'

Everyone was stunned by Cushapo's declaration, except Apo Kushak, who smiled and said, 'Very well, Cushapo, you may go now, and be sure not to miss any of your scenes.'

Cushapo happily jumped out of the room, which had neither a door nor a ceiling.

NINE

An Angel's Hand

IN THE MOUNTAIN village of Kadanga, the church was jam-packed. Inside, all the pews were filled, and some people were standing at the back. On the third row of the left aisle, Lisa's two smooth, tiny hands were clasped together in prayer, as if she had only one purpose in this world – to pray. She was only nine years of age, yet she knew all the hymns and prayers recited in her local church.

As the service was coming to its end, Lisa remained very still in her wheelchair. Her eyes were closed as she mumbled her final prayers. A hand softly touched her arm. Startled, she opened her eyes. Standing in front of her was an elderly priest, whom she had not seen for over a year.

A year ago, the priest had suffered a stroke, from which he was still recuperating. He was an extraordinary friend and had been there during her christening and birthdays. When she was six, the priest had visited her at the hospital almost every day for three weeks. He read her stories about apes and monkeys and tried to act the characters out, which made her laugh, despite her pain. Above all, he showed her how to express herself through prayer and encouraged her to write down her thoughts and feelings. Every day since then, Lisa had filled a page of her little pink diary with words and sketches. She had felt very sad when the priest fell ill at the age of eighty-five.

Now she cried, 'Oh, Father Eric, how are you? I'm so glad to see you again!'

People seated in the pews around Lisa stared at her, but she didn't notice. She was still talking to Father Eric, but he only touched her forehead and smiled radiantly. He then slowly walked away, his white robe barely touching the floor, as he faded from her view.

'Lisa?' whispered her mother, who was sitting next to her. She had heard Lisa talking on her own and was aware that people were staring.

The day before, Lisa's mother had heard that Father Eric had passed away. She couldn't bring herself to break the news to her daughter. Telling her now would surely devastate her. In her own little ways, Lisa had been trying hard to be independent. This morning, for the first time in over three years and without any assistance from anyone, she had got washed and dressed on her own, ready for the church service. Her mother smiled at this memory and recalled the first thing that Lisa had asked her this morning concerned a visit to the hairdressers.

The priest gave his final blessing and people started to make their way to the doors.

'Come on, darling, let's go to the hairdressers before they close,' the mother said, and she started to push Lisa's wheelchair towards the middle aisle and the door.

Lisa nodded, but she was preoccupied with why Father Eric had not spoken to her. Was she dreaming?

'*Mama*, shall I have my hair cut just below my shoulders,

with layers at the sides but no fringe at the front?' she asked as they crossed the road.

'Any way you want, darling,' replied her mother, who was casting her mind back four years earlier, to when they visited their relatives in the southern province.

It was beautiful then; Lisa was so active and energetic. The mother smiled as she recalled Lisa clad in her tiny yellow bikini, splashing water on the beach with her young cousins. A few weeks after they came back from that visit, Lisa's health slowly began to deteriorate. They thought it was flu at first, but then she had gastrointestinal symptoms, accompanied by a fever and muscle stiffness. It wasn't until several medical tests had been carried out that the doctors diagnosed poliomyelitis (polio). Her mother decided to give up her job to care for her daughter. They'd made numerous, gruelling trips to the hospital, with constant ups and downs.

Despite her condition, Lisa remained focused, which made her parents extremely proud. She still went to school, and everyone was hugely supportive of her. Also, she secretly enjoyed the special attention given to her by her friends and teachers.

The incident at the church kept coming back to Lisa's mother, and as they left the hairdressers, she decided that it was best to let her daughter know about Father Eric's death.

To her surprise, Lisa replied with a smile, '*Mama*, I think Father Eric came to give me his blessing this morning, when he put his hand to my forehead, which was also his special way of saying goodbye.'

TEN

A Life Beyond

SAMUEL BREATHED HIS LAST; his body lay peacefully on his bed as his family and friends gathered around to pay their last respects.

A womanly being arrived and led him up to a colourful spinning tunnel. He felt very light and bouncy, as he was lifted by the warmth of the wind that carried him and the woman to the tunnel. As they passed along the way, he could glimpse the stages of his previous life on earth.

When at last they came out to a very bright and cloudless space, they were led by dozens of angels down to a path surrounded by beautiful gardens, and he could smell the sweet scent of his wife's favourite perfume amongst the flowers.

The woman ushered him towards an ascending step. Their destination was a room with no walls, ceiling or floor, yet it was a bright, welcoming space of togetherness.

He was bewildered for some time as he wondered where he was. He couldn't see himself but felt the presence of other beings around him. They all seemed healthy and happy, and the atmosphere was calm, quiet and peaceful. They understood one another without uttering any words. Samuel eventually felt at home.

A year earlier, Samuel had been diagnosed with cancer of the pancreas. It was a big blow to his young family. How could he have developed such an illness at this early age? But then it could have been caused by all those years of abusing cigarettes, alcohol and drugs. Since his marriage six years ago, he had left all those vices behind, and he had started to enjoy life with his beautiful wife Rose and his now five-year-old daughter Lily Ann.

Following his diagnosis, Samuel stopped working and Rose had to give up her part-time job to take care of him and their daughter. It was a blessing that he had a critical illness insurance payout, which made his family financially secure. Samuel had to undergo immense therapy and various medical treatments. Still, amidst all the challenges and sometimes constraints his condition put on the family, they spent happy moments together and shared one another's little joys and sorrows. Then last month, he lost his fight for life, leaving his wife and daughter devastated.

Now, he could only watch over them; how he wished they could sense his presence around them.

'*Mama*,' called Lily Ann, who was looking up at the sky through her bedroom window.

'Yes, my dear?' answered Rose.

'Remember what *papa* said before he died, that whenever we miss him, we should look for the brightest, most twinkly star up in the sky, and that will be him?'

Lily Ann was very excited.

'Oh, yes,' replied Rose, as she joined Lily Ann at the window.

'Well, see right there,' she said, pointing to the far left side of the sky. 'I have been looking out for the brightest star, and there it is!' she exclaimed. She jumped up, as if trying to reach for the star. 'Mama, God has answered my prayers!'

Rose held her by the shoulders, looked into her eyes and hugged her tight. 'Yes, my child, your *papa* would have been forty-two years old tomorrow.'

Tears were rolling down Rose's cheeks, as they stood by the window, hugging each other while staring up at the sky.

If only they could feel the warmth around them; Samuel was hugging them both, too.

As he floated about the house, he pondered how he could go to different places simultaneously. He did not feel pain anymore, and he was happy where he was. He enjoyed the company of his family, whom he had not seen for many years. He had learned through them how to live his new life. Sometimes, he felt sorrowful when he saw his loved ones on earth crying, and he wished he could do something to make them happy again.

He recalled the day he and Rose got married in the village chapel. Rose, who was three months pregnant at the time, looked so beautiful in a stunning and elegant long white dress. He was wearing a traditional *barong* and a pair of black trousers, but everyone had their eyes on Rose, especially his best man, Mark.

'You know, Samuel, you are the luckiest man here on

earth, and I wish you and Rose the best of times together. Do take care of her,' Mark said to Samuel after the ceremony, and he promised Mark he would do his best for Rose.

They all grew up together in the mountain village of Palgaw. Later, Mark went to study engineering in the city while Samuel stayed in their town and trained in agriculture and farming, in the nearby town of Galat. Rose studied at the same college as Samuel and went on to become a midwife.

Both Samuel and Mark fell in love with Rose, but she chose to be with Samuel. However, the two men remained good friends. Soon after the wedding, Mark left the country to work for an engineering firm in the Middle East. He only returned for special occasions.

A knock at the door startled Rose and Lily Ann. They slowly walked towards the main entrance. There was another knock.

'Hello, it's just me, Mark,' called a familiar voice from outside.

Both Rose and Lily Ann's face lit up.

'Oh *mama*, it's *ninong* Mark!' Lily Ann exclaimed, as Rose opened the door.

'I'm so sorry to come here so very late in the evening,' said Mark, as he handed a bunch of flowers to Rose and a tiny, beautiful pink box to Lily Ann.

Lily Ann kissed him, while Rose hugged him.

'I wasn't able to come for Samuel's funeral, as I was tied up with a building construction in Qatar and didn't get the news until the day itself,' explained Mark to Rose as they sat in the living room. Lily Ann played happily with the music box that Mark had just given her.

'Don't worry, I'm sure Samuel understands . . . oh, we miss him so much, and Lily Ann talks about him all the time.'

Rose started to cry, and Mark hugged her.

'You know, I've decided to give up my work in the Middle East and move back here.'

Rose and Lily Ann looked at Mark in disbelief.

'That's great, Uncle Mark! Can I see you more often, then?' asked Lily Ann with hopeful eyes.

'Every day if you want,' he replied, as he picked her up and gave her a big cuddle.

Samuel smiled as he watched the three of them together. He could now sit back and relax knowing that his two beloved ones would be looked after by his best friend. But he would be watching over them for the rest of their lives on earth.

In the meantime, he could go for some adventures that he never had the chance to do while on earth. He planned to go to places in the Pacific, America, Africa, Europe and Asia. He wanted to see the Egyptian pyramids and even travel to Mars and Pluto. Oh, his list was endless!

Glossary

ama – dialect term for father, or sometimes grandfather or an elderly male relative.

ancicet – a form of an elf.

anting-anting – a magic token of any form, believed to give a supernatural power to the beholder.

basi – a fermented alcoholic drink made of sugarcane; the sugarcane is crushed and the juice is extracted, boiled and stored in large jars made of clay.

carabao – a domesticated water buffalo; a very common sight in farms in most South East Asian countries.

dawak – a healing rite performed by a medium to cure a seriously ill person.

gong – a percussion instrument made from copper, which is held and beaten by a piece of wood or mallet.

ina – dialect term for mother, or sometimes

grandmother or an elderly female relative.

kakarading – a superstitious belief that the spirits of dead ancestors and relatives exist.

Lola – used to address a grandmother or an elderly female relative, influenced by the Spanish language.

mama – mother, influenced by the Spanish language.

mandadawak – a local healer.

ninong – a godfather.

nipa hut – a hut with a thatched roof made of nipa palm leaves, and with walls and floors made of bamboos.

nipa palm – an unusual tree plant that has a horizontal trunk that grows beneath the ground; only the leaves and flower stalk grow upwards above the surface.

palok – a festival dance in the highlands of the Philippines, which consists of groups of male and female dancers; the males provide the music, each using a gong, and the females balance baskets or clay pots on their heads as they dance and snake in between the males, following some symbolic routines about highland living.

papa – father; influenced by the Spanish language.

rattan – a vine-like plant with a very long, strong and thin stem; it can grow up to hundreds of metres long.

salisid – a form of highland dance dedicated to spirits to help cure an ill person.

tungatong – music played using gongs when a person is ill; it is normally accompanied with the salisid dance.

About the Author

Emikat Jun was born in the highlands of the Philippines. From a very young age, she was fond of listening to folktales and other stories narrated to her by older relatives and friends.

Emikat gained an accounting degree in the Philippines before moving to the UK in 1995, where she worked in finance. While working and raising a child as a single parent, after her first marriage failed, she found time to pursue her childhood passion and studied for a degree in

English Language and Literature. She went on to gain her master's in MLitt Highlands and Islands Literature.

Today, *Emikat* lives in Coatbridge, Scotland, UK. Since her move to the UK, she has travelled to the Philippines several times to visit relatives and friends. Her debut novel, *Behind the Mask*, which was published in 2018, is set in the Philippines.

Printed in Great Britain
by Amazon